This book belongs to:

_____

To the memory of our wonderful cat Tex
and my mother-in-law's goldfish.

This paperback edition first published in 2013 by Andersen Press Ltd.

First published in Great Britain in 2012 by Andersen Press Ltd.,

20 Vauxhall Bridge Road, London SW1V 2SA.

Published in Australia by Random House Australia Pty.,

Level 3, 100 Pacific Highway, North Sydney, NSW 2060.

Text and illustrations copyright © Michael Foreman, 2012

The rights of Michael Foreman to be identified as the

author and illustrator of this work have been asserted by him

in accordance with the Copyright, Designs and Patents Act, 1988.

All rights reserved.

Colour separated in Switzerland by Photolitho AG, Zürich.

Printed and bound in Singapore by Tien Wah Press.

Michael Foreman has used watercolours in this book.

10   9   8   7   6   5   4   3   2   1

British Library Cataloguing in Publication Data available.

ISBN 978 1 84939 415 4

This book has been printed on acid-free paper

FRIENDS

MICHAEL FOREMAN

ANDERSEN PRESS

I'm lucky.
I'm a cat.
I can wander wild and free,
far and wide.

Poor old Bubble.
He's a fish . . .
Stuck in his tank.

He swims round and round,
down to the bottom, up to the top.
Then he swims round and round the other way.

Then he just looks at me and sighs.
He is my friend. He breaks my heart.

One day, when I was wandering wild and free,
I had a thought . . .

The bucket gave me an idea.

"Come on, Bubble. Jump!"

"Well done!"

I took Bubble to the pond in the park.
His eyes grew big and round.

He sighed and marvelled at the ducks and flying geese,
and the shadowy fish swimming among the water lilies.
He sighed . . .

"You've seen nothing yet," I said.

Then I took him to the river. His eyes grew even bigger. He had never seen so much water!

Then we followed the river to the wide, wide sea.

We watched the waves rolling in from the horizon,
and the shoals of fish swimming in the dark depths.

"Go on, Bubble," I said. "Dive in.
Be wild and free!"

But he looked at me and this time he didn't sigh.
He shook his head . . . and smiled a bubbly smile.
"Let's go home," he said.
"There may be lots of other fish in the sea,
but I might never find a friend like you."

So now we wander wild and free,
together, to the pond, the river and the sea.

Sometimes we wander the hills and
woods above the city . . .

and, on wet days, we explore
the great city itself.

Bubble and me
Have a world to see
From here . . .

To the rainbow's end.

Other books illustrated by Michael Foreman:

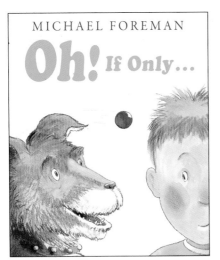

9781849393836

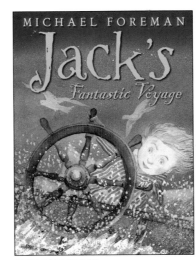

9781849392563

9781849392242

9781842705780

9781849392198

9781842709344